Pronunciation Guide

In Japanese:

a   always sounds like it does in the word "f**a**ther."
e   always sounds like it does in the word "m**e**t."
i   always makes an ee sound, like the word "s**ee**d."
o   always sounds like it does in the word "p**o**st."
u   always sounds like it does in the word "bl**ue**."

Most of the consonants sound the way they do in the English language, but there are a few things to remember:
The letter **g** always sounds like it does in the word "good."
The **f** sound is softer in Japanese than it is in English. When making an **f** sound, don't let your teeth touch your bottom lip; just blow.
Japanese doesn't have an **l**, **v**, **q** or **x** sound.

The Tuttle Story: "Books to Span the East and West"

Most people are very surprised to learn that the world's largest publisher of books on Asia had its beginnings in the tiny American state of Vermont. The company's founder, Charles E. Tuttle, belonged to a New England family steeped in publishing. And his first love was naturally books—especially old and rare editions.

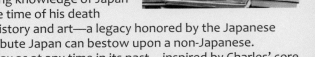

Immediately after WW II, serving in Tokyo under General Douglas MacArthur, Tuttle was tasked with reviving the Japanese publishing industry, and founded the Charles E. Tuttle Publishing Company, which still thrives today as one of the world's leading independent publishers.

Though a westerner, Charles was hugely instrumental in bringing knowledge of Japan and Asia to a world hungry for information about the East. By the time of his death in 1993, Tuttle had published over 6,000 titles on Asian culture, history and art—a legacy honored by the Japanese emperor with the "Order of the Sacred Treasure," the highest tribute Japan can bestow upon a non-Japanese.

With a backlist of 1,500 books, Tuttle Publishing is as active today as at any time in its past—inspired by Charles' core mission to publish fine books to span the East and West and provide a greater understanding of each.

Published by Tuttle Publishing, an imprint of Periplus Editions (HK) Ltd.

www.tuttlepublishing.com

Library of Congress Cataloging-in-Publication Data

Wright, Danielle.
  Japanese nursery rhymes : Carp streamers, Falling rain, and other traditional favorites / by Danielle Wright ; illustrated by Helen Acraman ; [translations by Anna Yamashita Minoura]. – 1st ed.
      v. cm.
  Summary: Traditional Japanese verses depicting the natural world and the many tiny moments that make childhood special, such as blowing bubbles, escaping the rain, rolling an acorn, or flying a kite. Presented in Japanese script, Japanese romanized form, and English.
  Contents: Hometown / by Tatsuyuki Takano – The roly-poly acorn / by Nagayoshi Aoki – The village festival / by Japan's Ministry of Education – Chorus of the raccoons / by Ujou Noguchi – Falling rain / by Hakushuu Kitahara – Little red bird / by Hakushuu Kitahara – Bubbles / by Ujou Noguchi – Train – Come spring / by Gyofuu Souma – Carp streamers / by Miyako Kondo – The seagull sailors / by Toshiko Takeuchi – Snow / by Japan's Ministry of Education – The rabbit's dance / by Hakushuu Kitahara – Moon / by Japan's Ministry of Education – The cradle lullaby / by Ujou Noguchi.
  ISBN 978-4-8053-1188-2 (hardcover)
1. Nursery rhymes, Japanese. 2. Children's poetry, Japanese. [1. Nursery rhymes. 2. Japanese language materials–Bilingual.] I. Acraman, Helen, ill. II. Minoura, Anna Yamashita III. Title.
  PZ8.3.W9317Jap 2012
  398.8–dc23
                    2011022776

ISBN 978-4-8053-1188-2

Distributed by

North America, Latin America & Europe
Tuttle Publishing, 364 Innovation Drive, North Clarendon, VT 05759-9436 U.S.A. Tel: 1 (802) 773-8930; Fax: 1 (802) 773-6993
info@tuttlepublishing.com; www.tuttlepublishing.com

Japan
Tuttle Publishing, Yaekari Bldg., 3rd Floor, 5-4-12 Osaki, Shinagawa-ku, Tokyo 141-0032. Tel: (81) 3 5437-0171; Fax: (81) 3 5437-0755
sales@ tuttle.co.jp; www.tuttle.co.jp

Asia Pacific
Berkeley Books Pte. Ltd., 61 Tai Seng Avenue #02-12, Singapore 534167. Tel: (65) 6280-1330; Fax: (65) 6280-6290
inquiries@periplus.com.sg; www.periplus.com

First edition   15 14 13 12 11   5 4 3 2 1   1109EP   Printed in Hong Kong

Japanese Nursery Rhymes

Carp Streamers, Falling Rain

and other traditional favorites

Danielle Wright

Illustrated by

Helen Acraman

TUTTLE Publishing

Tokyo | Rutland, Vermont | Singapore

Contents

All translations by Anna Yamashita Minoura.
Additional translation support from Manu & Erina at Team Yum Yum.

Introduction

Wherever in the world there are mothers and fathers, aunts and uncles, grandmothers and grandfathers, there are nursery rhymes. These traditional verses and songs have endured every fad and fashion imaginable over hundreds of years to remain a favorite part of childhood, continuing to create magical moments between children and parents.

When my son was a few weeks old, I searched for nursery rhymes from around the world and found quirky, touching, funny and heartfelt children's songs he loved – ones that didn't have gruesome endings like some of the Mother Goose rhymes I was familiar with. Each country I researched offered unique verses that spoke directly of its culture.

In Japanese nursery rhymes I found very beautiful and delicate verses with an emphasis on the natural world and dedicated to the many tiny moments that make childhood special, such as blowing bubbles, escaping the rain, watching an acorn roll or flying a kite.

Warabe Uta are traditional Japanese nursery rhymes and are often sung as part of traditional children's games, while Dōyō are more modern children's songs that were sung in compulsory music classes in primary schools around the country, and are closely tied to nature. This book includes selections of both types of rhyme.

There are three kinds of symbols used in written Japanese: Kanji (complex Japanese symbols originally from China), Hiragana characters (simple, rounded Japanese symbols developed in Japan) and Katakana characters (simple, angular Japanese symbols derived from kanji) – these last two are referred to as Kana. You will see all three types of writing in the pages of this book.

The verses are presented in an interlinear format to facilitate language learning, but Japanese text is normally written top to bottom, in columns right to left.

The rhymes are brought to life by the illustrations, the musical arrangements and the beautiful voices singing in both Japanese and English. I hope you enjoy reading, listening to, and singing these favorite Japanese rhymes.

With best wishes,
Danielle Wright

My Hometown*

故郷 Furusato

兎追いし　かの山
Usagi oishi ka no yama
The mountain where I chased rabbits

小鮒釣りし　かの川
Kobuna tsurishi ka no kawa
The river where I fished for carp

夢は今も　めぐりて
Yume wa ima mo megurite
The memories remain in me

忘れがたき　故郷
Wasure gataki furusato
I can never forget my hometown

如何に在ます　父母
Ika ni imasu chichi haha
How are you, Mother and Father?

恙なしや　友がき
Tsutsuga nashi ya tomogaki
I wonder if my old friends are well

雨に風に　つけても
Ame ni kaze ni tsuketemo
Even when rain falls and wind blows

思い出ずる　故郷
Omoi izuru Furusato
All I can think of is my hometown

志を　はたして
Kokorozashi o hatashite
Someday, I will pursue my dream

いつの日にか　帰らん
Itsuno hi nika kaeran
And return to my hometown

山は青き　故郷
Yama wa aoki furusato
Where the mountains are green

水は清き　故郷
Mizu wa kiyoki furusato
And the water is clear

如何に在ます　父母
Ika ni imasu chichi haha

志を　はたして
Kokorozashi o hatashite

*A Dojou is actually a Loach, an eel-like fish that stays close to the bottom of the pond or fish tank.

The Roly-poly Acorn
どんぐりころころ Donguri koro koro

どんぐり　コロコロ ドンブリコ
Donguri koro koro donburiko
A little acorn rolled and fell - splosh!

おいけに　はまって さあたいへん
Oike ni hamatte saa taihen
Right into a lake, oh no! What now?

どじょうが　でてきて こんにちは
Dojou* ga dete kite konnichiwa
A little fish appeared and said "hello"

ぼっちゃん　いっしょに あそびましょう
Bocchan issho ni asobimashou
"Little acorn, let's play together"

どんぐり　コロコロ よろこんで
Donguri koro koro yorokonde
The roly-poly acorn was so glad

しばらく　いっしょに あそんだが
Shibaraku issho ni asonda ga
And for a little while was having fun

やっぱり　おやまが こいしいと
Yappari oyama ga koishii to
But in the end he missed his home

ないては　どじょうを こまらせた
Naite wa dojou o komaraseta
And began to cry, making the fish sad

The Village Festival*

村祭　Muramatsuri

村の鎮守の神様の
Mura no chinju no kami sama no
Our village guardian god's generosity

今日はめでたい御祭日
kyou wa medetai omatsuri bi
Is what we celebrate on this joyous day

どんどんひゃらら　どんひゃらら
Don don hyarara don hyarara
Boom boom, whistle whistle

どんどんひゃらら　どんひゃらら
Don don hyarara don hyarara
Boom boom, whistle whistle

朝から聞こえる笛太鼓
asa kara kikoeru fue taiko
The flute and drum are heard from morning

*Japan has a number of different harvest festivals. In these celebrations, the first fruits of the harvest are offered to the gods of the fields as a token of thanks and to pray for good future harvests. Flutes, drums and bells are played, and dancing and processions take place.

年も豊年満作で
Toshi mo hounen mansaku de
This year we had a plentiful harvest

村は総出の大祭
Mura wa soude no oomatsuri
And the entire village is in full festivity

どんどんひゃらら　どんひゃらら
Don don hyarara don hyarara
Boom boom, whistle whistle

どんどんひゃらら　どんひゃらら
Don don hyarara don hyarara
Boom boom, whistle whistle

夜までにぎわう宮の森
Yoru made nigiwau miya no mori
We all celebrate into the night

治まる御代に神様の
Osamaru miyo ni kami sama no
At the end of our guardian's reign

めぐみ仰ぐや村祭
Megumi aogu ya mura matsuri
We are thankful for all his blessings

どんどんひゃらら　どんひゃらら
Don don hyarara don hyarara
Boom boom, whistle whistle

どんどんひゃらら　どんひゃらら
Don don hyarara don hyarara
Boom boom, whistle whistle

聞いても心が勇み立つ
Kiitemo kokoro ga isami tatsu
The pounding beat gives me strength

*The Tanuki is actually a racoon dog, a canine that lives only in eastern Asia. There are many myths about the Tanuki. The Tanuki in this rhyme lived in the forest near the temple, and at night they would come out and drum on their bellies with their front feet while dancing on their hind feet.

Chorus of the Raccoons

証城寺の狸囃子
Shoujouji no Tanuki* Bayashi

証　証　証城寺　証城寺の庭は
Sho Sho Shoujouji, Shoujouji no niwa wa
At the Shojoji temple, in the garden

ツ　ツ　月夜だ　皆出て　来い来い来い
Tsu tsu tsuki-yo da, minna dete koi koi koi
It's a full moon and it's time to come out, come out!

己等の友達ァ ぽんぽこ　ぽんの　ぽん
Oira no tomodacha, pon poko pon no pon
Me and my raccoon friends beat our bellies

負けるな　負けるな 和尚さんに　負けるな
Makeru na, makeru na, osho-san ni makeru na
Don't give up, don't give in, to the monk in the temple

来い　来い　来い　来い　来い　来い
Koi koi koi koi koi koi!
come out, come out, come out, come out

皆出て　来い来い来い
Minna dete koi koi koi!
Everybody come out!

証　証　証城寺　証城寺の萩は
Sho Sho Shoujouji, Shoujouji no hagi wa,
At the Shojoji temple, in the moonlight

ツ　ツ　月夜に　花盛り
Tsu tsu tsuki-yo ni hanazakari.
The bush clover is in flower

己等は浮かれて ぽんぽこ　ぽんの　ぽん
Oira wa ukarete pon poko pon no pon
We are delighted and beat our bellies in joy

Falling Rain

あめふり Ame furi

雨 雨 ふれふれ 母さんが
Ame ame fure fure kaasan ga
Rain, rain falling from the sky

蛇の目で　おむかい　うれしいな
Ja no me* de omukai ureshiina
My mother will come with her umbrella

びっち　ぴっち　ちゃっぷ　ちゃっぷ
Picchi picchi chappu chappu
Splish splash, splish splash

らん　らん　らん
Ran ran ran
La la la

*The umbrella described in this rhyme is called "Ja no me"—snake's eye — because of the ring pattern spanning the umbrella's face.

かけましょ　かばんを　母さんの
Kakemasho kaban o kaasan no
As I put on my bag and catch up with mother

後から　ゆこゆこ　鐘が鳴る
Ato kara yuko yuko kane ga naru
I can hear the bells on my bag ring

びっち　ぴっち　ちゃっぷ　ちゃっぷ
Picchi picchi chappu chappu
Splish splash, splish splash

らん　らん　らん
Ran ran ran
La la la

あら　あら　あの子は　ずぶ濡れだ
Ara ara anoko wa zubunure da
Uh oh – that little girl is getting wet

柳の根かたで　泣いている
Yanagi no nekata de naite iru
She's crying under the willow tree

びっち　ぴっち　ちゃっぷ　ちゃっぷ
Picchi picchi chappu chappu
Splish splash, splish splash

らん　らん　らん
Ran ran ran
La la la

母さん　ぼくのを　かしましょか
Kaasan boku no o kashimasho ka
I will lend her my umbrella, Mother

君　君　この傘　さしたまえ
Kimi kimi kono kasa sashita mae
"Here, you can take mine"

びっち　ぴっち　ちゃっぷ　ちゃっぷ
Picchi picchi chappu chappu
Splish splash, splish splash

らん　らん　らん
Ran ran ran
La la la

ぼくなら　いいんだ　母さんの
Boku nara iinda kaasan no
I'm safe under Mother's big umbrella

大きな　蛇の目に　はいってく
Ookina jya no me ni haitte ku
There's plenty of room for me

びっち　ぴっち　ちゃっぷ　ちゃっぷ
Picchi picchi chappu chappu
Splish splash, splish splash

らん　らん　らん
Ran ran ran
La la la

The Little Red Bird
赤い鳥小鳥 Akai tori kotori

赤い鳥、小鳥、
Akai tori, kotori
Little bird, red bird

なぜなぜ赤い
Naze naze akai
Why oh why so red?

赤い実をたべた
Akai mi o tabeta
Because it ate a red fruit

白い鳥、小鳥、
Shiroi tori, kotori
Little bird, white bird

なぜなぜ白い
Naze naze shiroi
Why oh why so white?

白い実をたべた
Shiroi mi o tabeta
Because it ate a white fruit

青い鳥、小鳥、
Aoi tori, kotori
Little bird, blue bird

なぜなぜ、青い
Naze naze aoi
Why oh why so blue?

青い実をたべた
Aoi mi o tabeta
Because it ate a blue fruit

Bubbles

シャボン玉
Shabon Dama

シャボン玉飛んだ　屋根まで飛んだ
Shabon dama tonda yane made tonda
The bubble I blew flew up to the roof

屋根まで飛んで　こわれて消えた
Yane made tonde kowarete kieta
But it burst as soon as it got there

シャボン玉消えた　飛ばずに消えた
Shabon dama kieta tobazu ni kieta
The bubble disappeared, but it didn't float away

生まれてすぐに　こわれて消えた
Umarete sugu ni kowarete kieta
It burst as soon as it was born

風　風　吹くな　シャボン玉飛ばそ
Kaze kaze fuku na shabon dama tobaso
Hush wind, don't blow, let us blow bubbles

The Train

汽車 Kisha

今は山中、今は浜、
Ima wa yamanaka ima wa hama
Now at the mountains, then the seashore

今は鉄橋渡るぞと、
Ima wa tekkyou wataru zo to
Next we cross the rail bridge

思う間も無く、トンネルの
Omou ma mo naku tonneru no
Passing through a dark tunnel

闇を通って広野原
Yami o tootte hiro nohara
And out into an open field

18

遠くに見える村の屋根、
Tooku ni mieru mura no yane
I can see rooftops of houses far away

近くに見える町の軒
Chikaku ni mieru machi no noki
And rows of houses nearby

森や林や田や畠、
Mori ya hayashi ya ta ya hatake
Forests and rice fields and farms

後へ後へと飛んで行く
Ato e ato e to tonde yuku
Flying by one after another

回り燈篭の絵のように、
Mawari dourou no e no you ni
Like the pictures on a spinning lantern

変わる景色のおもしろさ
Kawaru keshiki no omoshiro sa
The scenery changes so fast – what fun!

見とれてそれと知らぬ間に、
Mitorete sore to shiranu ma ni
Only a moment to admire the view

早くも過ぎる幾十里
Hayaku mo sugiru ikujuuri
At a million miles a minute

Come Spring

春よ来い　Haru yo koi

春よ来い　早く来い
Haru yo koi hayaku koi
Come spring, come soon

あるきはじめた　みいちゃんが
Aruki hajimeta Mii chan ga
Little Mii has just started walking

赤い鼻緒の　じょじょはいて
Akai hanao no jojo* haite
She wants to wear her red strapped sandals

おんもへ出たいと　待っている
Ommo e detai to matte iru
And go outside to play

春よ来い　早く来い
Haru yo koi hayaku koi
Come Spring, come soon

おうちの前の　桃の木の
Ouchi no mae no momo no ki no
The peach tree in our front garden

蕾もみんな　ふくらんで
Tsubomi mo minna fukurande
Is covered with plump buds

はよ咲きたいと　待っている
Hayo sakitai to matteiru
That are waiting to blossom

*Mii's hanao no jojo are probably the flat, thonged sandals also known as Zouri. Flip-flops are an imitation of this Japanese style.

Carp Streamers*

こいのぼり Koinobori

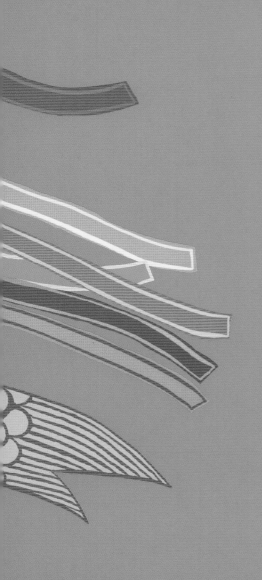

やねよりたかい　こいのぼり
Yane yori takai koinobori
Carp streamers fly high above the roof

おおきいまごいは　おとうさん
Ookii magoi wa otoosan
The black one is the father

ちいさいひごいは　こどもたち
Chiisai higoi wa kodomo tachi
The red ones are the children

おもしろそうに　およいでる
Omoshirosou ni oyoideru
All swimming happily in the air

みどりのかぜに　さそわれて
Midori no kaze ni sasowarete
Invited by the clean fresh wind

ひらひらはためく　ふきながし
Hira hira hatameku fuki nagashi
The colourful ribbons flutter

くるくるまわる　かざぐるま
Kuru kuru mawaru kazaguruma
And the pinwheel spins in circles

おもしろそうに　およいでる
Omoshirosou ni oyoideru
The carp swimming happily in the air

In Japan, the fifth day of the fifth month is Children's Day, a holiday set aside to celebrate the health and happiness of children. Carp streamers are flown because it's said that if a carp can swim upstream and reach a waterfall it becomes a dragon. The carp represents determination and success.

The Seagull Sailors

かもめの水兵さん
Kamome no Suihei san

かもめの水兵さん
Kamome no Suihei san
The seagull sailors

ならんだ水兵さん
Naranda suihei san
Are all lined up

白い帽子　白いシャツ　白い服
shiroi boushi, shiroi shatsu, shiroi fuku
white hat, white shirt, white from head to toe

波にチャップ　チャップ　　うかんでる
Nami ni chappu chappu ukanderu
They float among the waves and bob on the surface

かもめの水兵さん　かけあし水兵さん
Kamome no suihei san, kakeashi suihei san
The seagull sailors are all in a hurry

白い帽子　白いシャツ　白い服
Shiroi boushi, shiroi shatsu, shiroi fuku
White hat, white shirt, white from head to toe

波をチャップ　チャップ　越えてゆく
nami o chappu chappu koete iku
They float over the waves and move forward

かもめの水兵さん　ずぶぬれ水兵さん
Kamome no suihei san, zubunure suihei san
The seagull sailors are all wet

白い帽子　白いシャツ　白い服
Shiroi boushi, shiroi shatsu, shiroi fuku
White hats, white shirts, white from head to toe

波でチャップ　チャップ　　おせんたく
Nami de chappu chappu osentaku
They float in the waves and wash their clothes

かもめの水兵さん　なかよし水兵さん
Kamome no suihei-san, nakayoshi suihei-san
The seagull sailors, they are all good friends

白い帽子　白いシャツ　白い服
Shiroi boushi, shiroi shatsu, shiroi fuku
White hat, white shirt, white from head to toe

波にチャップ　チャップ　揺れている
Nami ni chappu chappu yurete iru
They float on the waves and sway

Snow

ゆき Yuki

雪やこんこ　霰やこんこ
Yuki ya konko arare ya konko
Fall snow, fall hail

降っては　降っては
Futte wa futte wa
As it keeps falling

ずんずん　つもる
Zun zun tsumoru
It piles up and up

山も野原も　綿帽子かぶり
Yama mo nohara mo wata boushi kaburi
The mountains and fields wear cotton wool hats

枯木残らず　花が咲く
Kareki nokorazu hana ga saku
The bare trees become covered in snowy flowers

雪やこんこ　霰やこんこ
Yuki ya konko arare ya konko
Fall snow, fall hail

降っても　降っても
Futte mo futte mo
No matter how much

まだ降り　やまぬ
Mada furi yamanu
It doesn't stop

犬は喜び　庭駆けまわり
Inu wa yorokobi niwa kake mawari
Dogs run around the garden with joy

猫はこたつで　まるくなる
Neko wa kotatsu* de maruku naru
Cats curl up beside the fireplace

*A kotatsu is actually a table that has a heating element on its underside. A quilt is draped over the table's sides to keep in the heat. Sitting with your legs and feet under the quilt will keep them warm.

The Rabbit Dance
兎のダンス Usagi no Dansu

ソソラ　ソラ　ソラ　兎のダンス
So sora sora sora usagi no dansu
Come watch, come watch the rabbits dance

タラッタ　ラッタ　ラッタ
Taratta ratta ratta
Hoppedy hop, hoppedy hop

ラッタ　ラッタ　ラッタ　ラ
Ratta ratta ratta ra
Hoppedy hop, hoppedy hop

脚で　蹴り蹴り
Ashi de keri keri
Kick, kick, kicking with their feet

ピョッコ　ピョッコ　踊る　耳に鉢巻
Pyokko pyokko odoru, mimi ni hachimaki∗
They jump, jump about, with bandannas on

ラッタ　ラッタ　ラッタ　ラ
Ratta ratta ratta ra
Hoppedy hop, hoppedy hop

ソソラ　ソラ　ソラ　可愛いダンス
So sora sora sora kawaii dansu
Come see, come see the adorable dance

タラッタ　ラッタ　ラッタ
Taratta ratta ratta
Hoppedy hop, hoppedy hop

ラッタ　ラッタ　ラッタ　ラ
Ratta ratta ratta ra
Hoppedy hop, hoppedy hop

とんで　跳ね跳ね
Tonde hane hane
Spring, spring, springing up high

ピョッコ　ピョッコ　踊る　脚に赤靴
Pyokko pyokko odoru, ashi ni akagutsu
They jump, jump about, wearing red shoes

ラッタ　ラッタ　ラッタ　ラ
Ratta ratta ratta ra
Hoppedy hop, hoppedy hop

*∗The bandanna these rabbits wear is a "hachimaki" —
a Japanese bandanna that is usually tied around the head.*

The Moon

月 Tsuki

でた　でた　つきが
Deta deta tsukiga
Look, look! The moon has risen

まるい　まるい　まんまるい
Marui marui manmarui
Round, round, so round

ぼんのような月が
Bon* no you na tsuki ga
Just like a round plate

かくれた雲に
Kakureta kumo ni
It has hidden behind the clouds

くろい　くろい　まっくろい
Kuroi kuroi makkuroi
Black, black, so black

すみのような雲に
Sumi no you na kumo ni
Just like dark ink

また　でた　つきが
Mata deta tsuki ga
Look! The moon has appeared again

まるい　まるい　まんまるい
Marui marui manmarui
Round, round, so round

ぼんのような月が
Bon no you na tsuki ga
Just like a round plate

The word "bon" is really "tray" in English.

The Cradle Lullaby

揺籠のうた　Yurikago no Uta

揺籠のうたを　カナリヤが歌うよ
Yurikago no uta o kanariya ga utau yo
A canary sings the cradle song

ねんねこ　ねんねこ　ねんねこよ
Nenneko nenneko nenneko yo
Hush, hush, hush now

揺籠のうえに　枇杷の実が揺れるよ
Yurikago no ue ni biwa* no mi ga yureru yo
Above the cradle loquat fruits sway

ねんねこ　ねんねこ　ねんねこよ
Nenneko nenneko nenneko yo
Hush, hush, hush now

揺籠のつなを　木ねずみが揺するよ
Yurikago no tsuna o kinezumi ga yusuru yo
Squirrels gently swing the cradle

ねんねこ　ねんねこ　ねんねこよ
Nenneko nenneko nenneko yo
Hush, hush, hush now

揺籠のゆめに　黄色い月がかかるよ
Yurikago no yume ni kiiroi tsuki ga kakaru yo
In your dream a yellow moon hangs in the sky

ねんねこ　ねんねこ　ねんねこよ
Nenneko nenneko nenneko yo
Hush, hush, hush now

*The loquat fruit, or biwa, is also known as the Japanese plum. This fruit is a distant relative of the apple.

Guide to the CD
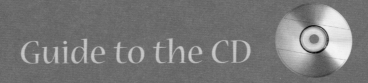

My Hometown
lyricist Tatsuyuki Takano • **composer** Teiichi Okano
Sung in Japanese by Jessica Rogers
Sung in English by Gabi Wannenburg

The Roly-poly Acorn
lyricist Nagayoshi Aoki • **composer** Tadashi Yanada
Sung in Japanese by Emma Sanders
Sung in English by Gabi Wannenburg

The Village Festival
lyricist Japan's Ministry of Education
composer Nouei Minami • Japan's Ministry of Education
Sung in Japanese by Jessica Rogers
Sung in English by Gabi Wannenburg

Chorus of the Raccoons
lyricist Ujou Noguchi • **composer** Shinpei Nakayama
Sung in Japanese by Emma Sanders
Sung in English by Gabi Wannenburg

Falling Rain
lyricist Hakushuu Kitahara • **composer** Shinpei Nakayama
Sung in Japanese by Emma Sanders
Sung in English by Gabi Wannenburg

The Little Red Bird
lyricist Hakushuu Kitahara • **composer** Tamezou Narita
Sung in Japanese by Emma Sanders
Sung in English by Gabi Wannenburg

Bubbles
lyricist Ujou Noguchi • **composer** Shinpei Nakayama
Sung in Japanese by Emma Sanders
Sung in English by Gabi Wannenburg

The Train
lyricist unknown • **composer** Aira Oowada
Japan's Ministry of Education
Sung in Japanese by Jessica Rogers
Sung in English by Gabi Wannenburg

Come Spring
lyricist Gyofuu Souma • **composer** Ryutaro Hirota
Sung in Japanese by Jessica Rogers
Sung in English by Gabi Wannenburg

Carp Streamers
lyricist Miyako Kondo *(first verse)*
composer unknown • **Sung in Japanese** by Emma Sanders
Sung in English by Gabi Wannenburg

The Seagull Sailors
lyricist Toshiko Takeuchi
composer Kouyou Kawamura
Sung in Japanese by Jessica Rogers
Sung in English by Gabi Wannenburg

Snow
lyricist & composer Japan's Ministry of Education
Sung in Japanese by Emma Sanders
Sung in English by Gabi Wannenburg

The Rabbit Dance
lyricist Ujou Noguchi • **composer** Shinpei Nakayama
Sung in Japanese by Jessica Rogers
Sung in English by Gabi Wannenburg

The Moon
lyricist & composer Japan's Ministry of Education
Sung in Japanese by Emma Sanders
Sung in English by Gabi Wannenburg

The Cradle Lullaby
lyricist Hakushuu Kitahara • composer Shin Kusakawa
Sung in Japanese by Jessica Rogers
Sung in English by Gabi Wannenburg

All music arranged and performed by Alex Borwick, borwick.alex@gmail.com • **Vocal supervisor:** Kim Wannenburg
Producer: Kenny MacDonald at www.macsroom.com • **Executive producer:** Danielle Wright, www.itsasmallworld.co.nz